What is That Noise?

For Claude,
Philipp and Alexander

Michèle Lemieux

What is
That Noise?

METHUEN CHILDREN'S BOOKS
London

'Oh, I'm so tired!' said the
big brown bear, waking from a deep sleep.
   'I was fast asleep, but I thought
I heard a noise – a funny
little noise. It's still going on.'

'What can it be?
It's not like the noise the mice make.
It's not so squeaky.
But now it has woken me up
and I can't get back to sleep.'

He stretched and yawned.
    'Have I slept all through the winter,
or just for one night?'
    The big brown bear felt very hungry.

'Listen!' said the bear. 'That funny noise
is still there.'
    But it wasn't the baby birds in their nest.
And it wasn't the frogs,
croaking down by the stream.

'I must find out what it is,' said the big
brown bear. 'I'll ask my friend, the tree.'
   'It's the woodmen,' said the tree.
'They are chopping down the forest.'

'Can you hear their axes?
They go chack, chack, chack.'

But the bear said: 'No, that's not my noise.
My noise is quite different.
It's not a chack, chack, chacky sort of noise.'

The bear went to ask the fish if he knew
what the noise was.

'Yes,' said the fish. 'It's the water-wheel
of the old mill, turning in the stream.
Can you hear it going creak-swish,
creak-swish?'

But the bear said: 'No, that's not my noise.
My noise is quite different.
It's not a creak-swishy sort of noise.'

Then the bear went to see if the
clever owl knew what the noise was.
She lived high up on a cliff.
She said to the bear:
'I don't know about your noise.
I only have ears for hunting.
Nothing else interests me.'

The big brown bear said to himself:
'Perhaps I shouldn't worry about the noise.
It is only a little noise, after all.
I can hardly hear it now.
Perhaps it's going away.'

Then the bear had a new idea.
He went to the farm, to see the farmer
and his wife picking fruit. There were
baskets full of lovely red tomatoes.
　　The greedy bear was fond of tomatoes.
He climbed a tree and threw apples down
into the duckpond. The ducks and geese
were frightened by the splashes,
and the farmer and his wife left
their baskets, to see what was happening.

Then the naughty bear ran quickly up and carried away
a whole basket of tomatoes while no-one was looking.

A little way off he sat down
behind a bush and started eating,
while the poor watchdog was given
a dreadful scolding.

   But then the noise came back,
and now it was like the thump,
thump, thump of a drum.

   'What can it be?' said the big brown bear.
'I don't like it.'

'Perhaps some honey would cheer me up,'
thought the bear. After all,
honey is what bears like best of all.'
So he decided to wait until it was dark
and everyone was inside.

Then it was time to creep quietly up to
the beehives, on soft, soft paws . . .

'Oh! Ouch!' The angry bees flew out and
stung the bear on his nose, where it hurt.

And then came the farmer, waving
his pitchfork.

The bear ran away, as fast as he could.
And as he ran he heard that noise again
– thump, thump, thump.

The night was cold and dark
as he set off for home.
    'Oh, dear,' he said.
'Now it's raining,
and my fur will get all wet.
Oh, oh! That was lightning,
and now thunder!
It's a real storm.
I must hurry back, as fast as
I can, to my dry, warm den.'

But what was that,
running close behind him?
It was the noise, again.
And yet, when the bear looked round,
no-one was there.
He was frightened.

Safely home in his cave at last.
But the noise was still with him,
only it was quieter now, and slower,
as if it was tired from running, too.
    'Brrr!' said the bear. 'It's cold,'
and he watched the sun come up.

The bear began to feel sleepy.
The birds were getting ready to fly south;
it was time for everyone to find winter quarters.

'Is that funny noise still there?'
The bear listened. Everything was quiet,
even the little mice who shared his den.
And then, at last, the bear knew where the noise came from.
    'It's inside me,' he thought.
'It's my heart, beating.
That's what it was, all the time!'

And now it was time for the bear's winter sleep.
Now not even the loudest noise could waken him.
    But one morning, when the snow has melted away,
the bear will wake from his long sleep,
and feel his heart beating once again,
and then he will know, all of a sudden, that . . .

. . . it is Spring again.

And the big brown bear will dance for joy.

And what about you?
The big brown bear
has a question for you.
Can you feel your heart
beating, there inside you?
    When you're happy and excited,
it goes fast;
and when you're tired and sleepy,
it goes slowly and sleepily too.

Can you hear it?
You have to be very quiet . . .
Shhh . . .

The Author

Michèle Lemieux lives in Canada, and grew up there, in a country where bears still roam in the wild. She went to art school in Montreal.

Ever since her own childhood she has wanted to tell and illustrate this story. Every child at some time shares the bear's moment of discovery when it first becomes aware of its own heart beating. It is one of the milestones on the road to self-discovery – a moment to treasure for ever afterwards.

First published in Great Britain in 1984
by Methuen Children's Books Ltd,
11 New Fetter Lane, London EC4P 4EE
Published in German by Otto Maier Verlag
under the title *Was hört der Bär?*
Text and illustrations copyright © 1984 by Otto Maier Verlag
English Translation by David Ross copyright © 1984
by Methuen Children Books Ltd
Printed in Italy

ISBN 0 416 49450 1